A Thamesfield Academy Drama

First published in Great Britain in 2020 by

Paper Pages Publishing Ltd.

All Rights Reserved

{The moral rights of the author have been asserted.}

Illustrations copyright © 2020 Ny M Jones
Text copyright © 2020 Ny M Jones
Design by Paper Pages Publishing Ltd
ISBN: 978-1-9164291-8-5

WWW.PAPERPAGESLTD.COM

DEDICATION

I dedicate this to my young Black British Teens, who have been overlooked and underrepresented.

We are Mystery, We are Comedy, We are Action, We are Thriller, We are Science-Fiction, We are Fantasy, We are Romance, We are Adventure, We are Horror, We are Contemporary, We are Fiction, We are Factual, We are Historical, We are Art, We are Poetry, We are All Things and should NEVER be defined by ONE.

READ - BELIEVE - ACHIEVE

CHAPTERS

ACKNOWLEDGEMENTS

I want to acknowledge the admin team for *"The School Reunion"* Whatsapp Group. This reconnection to my childhood allowed me to reflect on my teen years and my own reading experiences. I was a young black girl from the UK, saturated in American culture, with a hunger to see books that reflected my lifestyle, culture and peers. It is here that I also acknowledge the group members, **Cardinal Pole RC Class of 2002**, every single one of you has influenced my writing more than you will know and there is a small piece of each of you in the characters I have created.

I do wonder how different things would have been if we got to see behind each other's masks back then.

CHAPTER 1

CARLY WHO?

'Ouch! Excuse me, officer, can you please loosen these?'

I've already asked him twice. My cheek is killing me, and these cuffs are squeezing my wrists. When they had first arrested me, the big officer who is now guarding the door had tied my hands behind my back, then literally, dragged me across the field like I was some violent thug. I thought my shoulders were going to pop with the way he was pulling me. They probably would have by now, but the female officer who is here kept telling him to take it easy and insisted, when we get back to the house, my hands be placed in front. She kept saying to him that I was a minor, but he didn't seem to care. He continued to drag me towards the Manor house until just outside the entrance, I felt the cuffs release. Holding my right arm, he swung my left arm around to the front and retightened them. Even though he continued to pull me until I sat down, my shoulders were now cool, but as for my wrists...... They need prayer.

For some weird reason, I get the vibe that he doesn't like me or really believes I'm a murderer.

Just look at how he is staring at me!

I know I should keep focus, but I can't lie, I am surprised to see that these handcuffs look nothing like the ones in my little brother's toy box. There is no little release clip on the side and the small chain that holds the cuffs together is actually a big black rectangular block. It's about the length of a small ruler and I don't see the point of it. It's like an annoying wedge that is social-distancing my hands for no reason, and every time I flex to scratch my fingers, my wrist literally feels as if it's about to break.

But seriously; Why am I being arrested when she attacked me? If you look good, I'm sure, you can see her handprint on my face. But I swear, I didn't push her. I don't know what the hell happened. I think it was an accident. What I do know is, she hit me, I tried to block it, then she grabbed her head and fell. I don't know if something or someone hit her, but I definitely didn't.

That's it! Someone hit her, and they are blaming me as a cover-up. Why else would them lot say I pushed her?

It would be easy to believe, everyone knows that I am not her biggest fan; But other than the twins, who is? I just wish Taylor could've been there, she would have stopped all these lies. I don't like her, but I don't hate her. I didn't even want to hurt her, let alone kill her. Honestly, I am completely over the *"Damian Clark thing"* or whatever you want to call it, that was so year nine.

A few years ago, two to be precise, I liked this boy Damian Clark in the year above. In fact, most of the girls in my year did. Damian was what we called a *"Peng Ting"*. He had over 20k followers online, kept the freshest trim and his crep game was off the hook. Girls loved him, and guys envied. He had so many 'undercover haters' and frenemies, that there was always a rumour running with his name in it. They used to say that he didn't own the trainers he posted himself wearing and that the boxes in the background of his pictures were empty. It never actually bothered him because no one dared to say it to his face. But, there was this one time that someone had anonymously posted his picture online with the caption *"#bowwowchallenge"* which had got the whole school talking, and for the first time, I think it got to him.

The Bow Wow Challenge was an online joke about people who faked their lifestyles to look richer than they were. It had started with the celebrity *"Lil Bow Wow"*, hence the name "#bowwowchallenge". He had posted a picture of himself on a plane, with a caption that insinuated that he was on a private jet – 'living his best life', so to speak. At first, no one had questioned how genuine the post was because he was a celebrity. But a few comments in, fans began to call him out and accused him of lying. Many of them had been travelling on the same flight as him, which was in fact, an economy aeroplane. He had cleverly cropped the image to mislead his followers. Although he denied that was his intention, the photo went completely viral, for all the wrong reasons. He was trolled for weeks, as well as being the main topic on gossip blogs. Online users then created a challenge in which people posted themselves being deliberately deceptive for fun using the hashtag *"Bowwowchallenge"*.

Me and Taylor had even taken part. One Saturday afternoon, we went to a furniture showroom with my dad to get some new units for the church's kitchen and we decided to take some pictures inside the display rooms. Before posting on our pages, we cropped the images so that you could not see the edges of the exhibit walls, then added the caption: *When you and bestie get a new yard! #bowwowchallenge.* We got so many likes.

So, when the anonymous post first appeared on our school's profile page, with the image of Damian standing in front of his wall of shoe boxes and the caption #bowwowchallenge, everyone was talking about it, even teachers. That day was the first time I ever saw him look embarrassed or bothered. He never confronted anyone about it, I mean, he couldn't. But I do remember, to prove a point, he wore a different pair of trainers to school every day for a month afterwards; despite being banned from lessons for not wearing shoes.

Each morning, he would post a similar video clip. It always started with a selfie view of him licking his lips and winking, whilst the chorus of *'Soulja Boy's – Turn my swag on'* played as the backing track. The video would then change the camera view in cue with the line from the song, *'I'm getting money...'*, to show his trainers as he walked. He captioned each post with a made-up hashtag, *"#Stuntondemchallenge"*, which was his comeback to whoever had created or made banter at the Bow Wow Challenge post. He would get thousands of likes on each post and had even landed a sponsorship deal from *Puma* shortly afterwards.

I ain't got a clue what he's doing these days, but with hindsight, I actually can't believe I thought all that 'lip-licking' was cool. Like, he had mock exams that year and was unlikely to learn much from sitting, *'swagged up'*, outside a classroom. To think, I used to dream of one day becoming Mrs Clark, "hell to the no". For the record, my future husband needs to be someone smart, like Marlon, that kind of stupid just isn't cool to me anymore.

But at the time, all the girls in my form knew I liked him. I would put hearts with the initials *"D.C"* on the last page of all my workbooks. I had even got Taylor's aunty to do my hair in blonde lemonade braids which I rocked for a few months because he had posted a picture of Beyonce with the same hairstyle. I rinsed them so much that before I had taken them out, the partings had disappeared. But his caption was *"I need my wife to look like this,*

#Facts", and at the time I needed to be his wifey. So, obviously, when I originally got the phone call, I was gassed. It was a late evening and I had been chilling out at Taylor's when the phone rang. The conversation went something like this:

Hello

Is this Chenade?

Why? Who's this?

What? You don't recognise my voice?

[Kisses teeth] I beg you stop playing games or I'm hanging up

Chillout girl! Your so feisty, but it's why I like you

Seriously, you got about 3 more seconds before I hang....

Alright, damn. It's me, Damian.

Damian? [Heart rate increases]

Yeah, Clark. What's going on?

You alright? How did you get my number?

Don't worry about all that. Is it a prob...

No!

Then good. Not gonna lie, you've been looking mad decent lately, I'm feeling your hair still.

Really? I mean, Thanks.

Yeah man. I like you. What you saying though, do you have a man?

Noooooo!

So, are you chatting to next man?

Maybe [Giggle]

Well, if you are, bun dat and bun dem!

Let's link up. Are you on it?

Maybe

What's all this 'maybe'. Yes or No?

[Giggle] *Send me your number and I'll let you know when*

Why send it? Just put it in your phone. I'll give it to you now if you're ready.

One sec, let me put you on loudspeaker......Go on then

0-7-9-Never-in-life-would-he-like-you

[Group laughter]

Then the phone hung up.

To be honest, I knew something was dodgy about the phone call. Now I think about it, it blatantly wasn't his voice. But at the time, my mind was racing, and I wasn't thinking straight. As soon as it happened, I felt like such a mug. I just couldn't believe that someone would hate me that much that they would do that. Then the worst happened. About an hour later, both mine and Taylor's phone started to vibrate like crazy. When we checked our screens, I literally wanted to die. There were hundreds of notifications coming through, mostly laughing emojis. But as I scrolled further, beyond the *"Sad"* - ***cover ear emoji*** or *"Sounds so thirsty, water needed!"* - ***water drop emoji***, I saw it. I, Damian Clark and half of Thamesfield Academy were tagged in a post that was captioned ***"Chenade Loves Damian"***. When you clicked on the link, it played an audio recording of the entire prank call, and I had sounded so desperate. The next day at school everyone was talking about it. Through all the Chinese whispers, I had heard that Carly Rothman, the usual villain, had got her big brother, Anthony, to make the call, whilst her and 'The Minions' had recorded it.

When I confronted her a few times, she finally admitted the phone call but claimed that she had nothing to do with the online post. But through all the lying, one of the minions slipped up and practically admitted that it was them. By that point, I had had it, I didn't care who said or did what, I just wanted to beat up Carly and her dumb friends. Luckily for them, Taylor kept reminding me that *'karma'* was a real thing, and she could personally ensure they would eventually get what they deserved.

She was right. Not that I wanted Carly dead, but about the whole *'karma'* thing. I guess it just wasn't how I anticipated. I'll admit, I was mad with her for about a week after the prank, then it was like *"Carly who?"*.

Literally, every week at Thamesfield someone else becomes a new victim of Carly and last week's drama is forgotten. She can be a proper bitch, so I have purposely kept my distance over the years. So, room allocation this afternoon, was the first time in ages that I had actually acknowledged she even existed.

Like I said before, *'Carly Who?'*.

CHAPTER 2

CHENADE'S STORY

Today I got up at 5am. My form tutor Ms Strauss had given strict instructions for us to arrive at school by 6.30am, as it was a 6-hour coach drive to the residential. I must have been excited to go because I did not snooze my alarm clock once. By 5.30am my suitcase was packed, and I was showered and dressed. I had put on my pink Converse hoody, with my pink Converse trainers and had slicked my hair into a high bun. I spent at least fifteen minutes and half a tub of edge control making sure my baby-hairs were laid perfect. The lighting in the bathroom had me feeling myself, so I decided to take a few selfies and posted my favourite one online with the caption, *"Pretty in Pink"*.

I then went downstairs and grabbed breakfast. My mum had got up extra early to fry me some dumplings, plantains, scrambled eggs and beans, my favourite. She said I needed to eat something 'proper' because for the next four days I would be, in her words, '*yamming foolishness*'.

I sat and scrolled my updates as I ate and waited for Taylor and her dad to pick me up. The Wesley Twins, who me and Taylor refer to as '*Carly's Minions*', had just posted a video of themselves riding suitcases on their driveway, wearing some '*butterz*' tracksuits. The video wasn't even funny either. The clip started with the pair walking into view, dragging their suitcases behind them. They then turned around in complete unison, blew a kiss at the camera and said their trademark catchphrase '*It's Twinidadian, Baby!*'. Then, after practically forcing Shana to sit on her suitcase, Shayla attempted to mount hers. She looked so awkward because she was unnecessarily contorting her shoulders to get her bum in the camera view. She then called out, '*Marks! Set! Go!*'. As she thrusts herself forward there is a loud cracking sound, followed by hysterical laughter. Shayla then jumps off her suitcase. Whilst wiggling her head and pushing her open hand toward the lens, she starts cussing, '*I paid five-bills yuh nah!*'.

It was blatantly obvious that the suitcase couldn't hold their weight, so why even try? I think they just wanted to show off the fact that they were expensive and designer. They would never miss an opportunity to let you know their dad had money.

Shayla and Shana have been following Carly around for as long as I've known them, but it wasn't until

Shana got moved up to my maths set this year, that I've been able to tell them apart. It doesn't help that they are always dressed the same and have their heads inside Carly's backside, but I can tell the difference because she has a more rounded nose. Although I have never really spoken to her, Shana is the one that most people prefer.

The Thamesfields Pits, Jake, Kai and Chris posted themselves walking to school in matching jackets. I had wondered why Marlon wasn't with them, as they are usually joined at the hips. We call them *'The Thamesfield Pits'* or *'The Pits'* because it was the name they had used in Year 7, for the *Thamesfield Talent Fest.* As the show finale, the four did an epic performance to the RnB classic, *Candy Rain,* and the band-name has stuck with them ever since. It was the first time in Thamesfield history that year 7s had closed the talent show, so it was a big deal.

I still remember it like it was yesterday. Halfway through their routine, they had ripped off their shirts, and the lead singer, Kai, dropped to his knees to seduce the crowd. He was whining his hips and running his hands through his dreadlocks. I swear, everyone went nuts. I'm pretty sure that every girl seated in the hall stood up and screamed when they had finished. The only thing missing to make their performance fully certified was some on-stage rainwater and flashing lights. It was literally the biggest performance anyone at Thamesfield had seen up until then and even had the year 11's talking about it. The foursome has been inseparable and coordinating outfits ever since and is why it felt so odd to see them without Marlon, especially for a trip this big.

Hayley-Rose, who calls herself '*The Ginger Nut*', had also posted. It was a picture of a suitcase filled with more alcohol than clothes, and I honestly don't know how she got all that packed without her mum seeing. Despite being nearly 16, my mum insisted on giving my case a once over this morning, meaning, I would never have got away with that. Besides, where would I get it? All the shopkeepers around here know my age and my Dad.

As planned, Taylor arrived at the door, wearing the blue version of my outfit, but her hair was styled differently. She had zig-zagged patterned braids at the front with her hair freshly straightened at the back. Her aunty had done her a *'Silk Press'* the night before. We never tried to match hairstyles as Taylor's hair is a different length and texture to mine.

As she helped me lug my suitcase to the boot of the car, her dad called out *"Hashtag Twinning!"* followed by laughter. We both dropped the suitcase and started laughing too. Although he can sometimes be a cringe, Taylor's dad is so cool. He is one of those liberal men who believe that Taylor should make all her own decisions. Despite being Grenadian, he was born in Britain, and culturally, has very "British" ideals of parenting and discipline. I wish he could befriend my parents because their stance is until I leave their home, they make the decisions and I don't have a choice. My parents are very *'old-school'* if you know what I mean. He, however, let us listen to anything we wanted, regardless of the lyrics, because he loved our music too. He is always taking us to music events as part of his job and gets us backstage passes to meet celebrities all the time. On the way, we stopped at the petrol station and he had brought us a load of snacks for the coach, including fizzy drinks, all because Taylor had insisted he buy them, despite Ms Strauss' specific warning that fizzy drinks were not allowed on the coach. I bet if it was my mum taking us, we probably wouldn't have got a drink, let alone them being fizzy.

To be fair my mum isn't too fond of Taylor, so she would never have offered the lift. She thinks there is something strange about her, and in her words *'the spirit doesn't take to her'*. But that's typical of my mum, she thinks everyone I talk to is strange or no good for me. My dad, on the other hand, doesn't share his opinion. He is a minister at ANCC, *The Afro Nations Community Church*, so it feels like his answer to everything is *'Thou shall not judge'* or prayer.

Disclaimer: I know Tay-Tay can be a little OCD, I'll admit, but she's my bestie and is more loyal than anyone I know.

As we arrived at school, the coach was already parked on the kerb with the doors open. I had noticed

Ms Strauss standing just outside with a clipboard and could see pupils already boarding. It's actually crazy how different some people look when they are not wearing a school uniform. As we got closer, I spotted Marlon sitting at the front of the coach in the seat behind the driver. *Disclaimer: I would notice that boy from a mile away. Marlon Christian-Thomas is so my type.*

Like in the video this morning, he wasn't with The Pits, so I assumed that he must be in trouble because no one ever sits that close to the front unless they are on punishment. Which is still odd as Marlon is a straight-A student. Either way, it felt strange. As we walked closer, I nudged Taylor's shoulder and giggled that today would be an exception to the *"front of the coach"* rule, as I wanted to sit as close to him as possible. But when we boarded, occupying the seats behind him, was Carly and her minions. So, I led Taylor straight to the empty seats at the back. We buckled up, put both earbuds in and inconspicuously sipped our fizzy.

The good thing was, the journey did not feel like 6hrs. I spent the whole time listening to podcasts and watching live feeds online. Luckily, the coach had a really good Wi-Fi connection. There was nearly a fight halfway through the journey, just after we had stopped for a toilet break, but I didn't even clock. I only found out later at lunch, when the girls at my table were talking about it, but I lost any interest once I heard Carly was involved.

Like I always say, '*Carly who?*'.

The Manor House we were staying in was on a Moor. The last ten minutes of the coach drive felt like we had left civilisation. All you could see through the windows were trees and hills. There were no pavements for people to walk and no visible street lights. I even asked myself, *could you imagine how scary it must look in the night?*

On arrival, we were greeted by a tall and frail-looking man, who introduced himself as the owner, Mr Coppin. His eyes were sunken inside the shrivelled skin on his face and his hair was pure white. Despite his look, his mannerism displayed a lot more youth than I had expected. He told us about the history of the building, health and safety, along with some other rules and regulations. The only rule I remembered was the "No Phone" rule, as we all had to label our phones and place them in a black bucket.

Strike One, I should have known from then, that this, was not going to be the trip I had in mind.

Ms Strauss followed by allocating us to our bedrooms. She did this in groups of 5, according to our surnames and as soon as she announced the process, I was vexed at the maths. Taylor's surname is "Henry" and mine is "Smith", so, unless those bodies on the coach were ghosts, I knew straight away we would not be in the same room.

Strike Two, 'No bestie'. There is no possible way things could get any worse.

But then, things took a turn for the worst when Ms Strauss called the names for Room 7. She first called Carly **R**othman and as soon as she did, I crumbled. I knew exactly where things were heading, as the next name called alphabetically was - *Chenade **S**mith*. Then Ashly **T**homas, the girl who doesn't speak. I swear, in the last five years, I've only ever heard her say "yes" to the register, so this should be interesting.

Then a *'could-my-luck-be-any-worse'* moment happened. Ms Strauss called the final two names for the room, Shana and Shayla **W**esley, aka *Carly's Minions*.

Strike Three, I really should have protested to leave. The trip was cursed!

I was basically stuck in a room with a mute, Satan, his helpers and no contact with the outside world. How on earth was I going to get through the next four days is all I could think. But standing here in handcuffs, I should have known we wouldn't even make it through the first night.

CHAPTER 3

ROOM 7

After having something to eat we were all sent to our rooms. Room 7 was a large L-shaped room. There were two sets of bunk beds against the back wall, and a single bed in the corner. To the left of the beds was a large mirrored cupboard and left of that was a small bathroom. On the far-right wall was a small, shoebox-sized window. It was covered with a dingy grey net curtain and had become translucent due to the amount of dirt.

The floors were covered in a flat brown, ribbed carpet and had a huge, ringed, watermark below the radiator. There were yellow streaks in the corners of the ceiling and another watermark not too far from the bathroom. Have you ever forgotten to hang out your swimming kit? That is what room 7 smelt like to me, with the added musk of strong cleaning fluid.

Ashly immediately sat on the single bed when we entered the room, I assumed this was her way of claiming it as hers. I could tell that it had irritated

Carly by the suck of her teeth and the screw-face she had pulled, but she knew if she had made an issue, she would have looked like a bully. So instead she muttered something to the twins that made them look over at Ashly and laugh. Shana then climbed to the top bunk of the first bed, whilst Carly sat on the bunk below, with Shayla standing next to her, leaning on the bedpost.

I was halfway climbing the second bunk bed, when I heard Shayla turn and say, about me, '*I would rather sleep top and tail with Shana, than beneath a sket!*'.

Little did she know, the feeling was mutual, but before I could react, Carly stood up. I didn't quite hear what she said, but it was something like, "______ *it! Shay, Chenade is* ______".
But whatever it was, it had sounded rude.

My eyebrows immediately narrowed, and my nostrils flared, as I sharply asked her to repeat what she had said. I needed to be sure of how to react. But she didn't repeat herself and instead, she got off the bed and walked towards me. I still couldn't read the expression on her face, so started to clench my fist in preparation for whatever was coming next. There was no way that I was about to get caught in one of Carly's attacks. But shockingly, she reached forward and shook my hand. She followed by saying, "*I'm willing to squash whatever it is if you are? I always thought you were cool, Chenade*".

Thinking this was another prank, I cautiously scanned the room. I looked over at Ashly whose eyes were wandering, then at Shayla whose eyes were fixated on Carly, then at Shana who was looking at me. She appeared pleasantly surprised. I then looked back at Carly, shrugged my shoulders and said *'Cool. At least I can now sleep with both eyes closed.'*

We both burst into laughter and she cheekily chuckled, *'Me too!'*

In that same moment, the door swung open. It was Hayley-Rose and a litre bottle of vodka. She charged over to Carly and shoved the bottle in her hand.

'Here you go.' She said. *'You were moving so stupid on the coach, you were gonna get us caught and I told you I was gonna buss you after, so here.'*

'No, not here Ginger Nut.' Said Carly shoving the bottle back in Hayley's hand. *'Let's go for a walk, I don't want it in the room. I am not tryna get caught if one of the teachers or that old guy, Mr Coffin, comes in here. If we're outside we can get rid of the evidence and at least, say it isn't ours. In here what are we gonna say? It's Ashly's? Yeah, right. Plus, we've got nearly three hours before dinner, so there is time to kill.'*

'I was just about to think you had turned moist Carly Rothman, but, No! You're still a bitch.' said Hayley and the two chuckled.

'Wait 5 minutes though, let us get changed first'

Ushering Hayley to the side with the back of her palm, Carly addressed the room, *'Girls put on all black, including you Ashly. Room 7 has to be the pengest, so hurry up and get changed!'*

And as if she had magical powers, we all went in our suitcases, pulled out something black and changed, including Ashly. When it comes to Carly, there is just something about her. Her physical beauty is immediately obvious, she is one of the prettiest girls in school. Her piercing hazel eyes, her flow of curly jet-black hair and deep cheek dimples, perfectly complement each other. She has the physique of a fitness model and the smile of an angel. But believe me, that's just on the outside. Despite her beauty, Carly gives pretty girls a bad name. She is probably the most manipulative and spiteful person at Thamesfield, with a bible-size CV of examples that extends back to year 7. She literally has the soul of a demon. I think people only bow down to her for an easy school life or out of fear, apparently, her older brother is a *'Roadman'*. But for whatever reason, at that moment, I was one of those people, one of Carly's minions. I had thanked god Taylor wasn't there to see it.

Carly took the lead and led us along the corridor, down the stairwell and out through one of the many exit doors. Outside we walked for about 15 minutes, with Hayley entertaining us along the way. We passed various groups hanging in and around the grounds. Behind the building was a group smoking and close by was another group playing music and drumming the beat on a bench. There were also a few people loitering around individually.

As we walked along the edge of the reservoir, we saw The Pits, but still no Marlon. They were skimming stones into the water to make ripples and Kai was cussing Hayley's singing. At one point she was trying to fight him and fell flat on her bum. We saw them again a little later, near the bushes, this time Marlon was there, looking even finer than he did this morning. They didn't notice us as they were still throwing stones, but now, they were concentrating as if there was a cash prize for the best throw, so we didn't say anything to them.

We managed to find a quiet spot on the other side of the bushes, and it was perfect. There were seven stumps in a circular arrangement under a tree, with the bushes shielding us from the view of the Manor House. We each took a seat on a stump and Carly took stage in the centre. She was holding the bottle of already mixed vodka that she had grabbed out of Hayley's hand seconds before. She opened it and took a swig. As soon as the bottle opened you could smell the aroma of alcohol immediately filling the air. She then passed it to Shayla, who passed it to Shana, then to Hayley who passed it to me. Hayley swigged as if she had just run a *cross country event* and it was a bottle of ice-cold water to quench her thirst. Like an idiot, I followed her lead and literally had to spit my first sip out. It probably put

Ashly off as she didn't drink any. Each time I passed the bottle to her, without hesitation, she passed it straight back to Carly. But as soon as the liquid touched my lips, I knew Hayley had to be drunk. It was too strong because despite what she had claimed, she had barely mixed any lemonade in it. Each time I drank I felt a sensation of heat travel through my chest into my stomach. By the third time the bottle came around, it didn't feel as bad, probably because by then, I was tipsy. To be honest, I think we all were. It felt as though it was the only thing helping us get through Carly's stories. Well, everyone except Hayley. You could clearly see that she was drunk by her random outbursts which were also annoying Carly, and at first, she really tried her best to ignore her.

But Hayley, as she does with everyone, began to call Carly a liar. As an example, she brought up the #bowwowchallenge incident with Damian Clark and accused Carly of being the one who had made the post. The annoyance on Carly's face grew, but Hayley kept getting louder as she gave more evidence for her claim. She then turned to me and said, '*Talking of Damian Clark, since when are you two friends after she mugged your life with that phone call?*'

That was it, Carly had had enough. Before I could answer, she told Hayley that if she didn't shut her mouth, she was going to do it for her. But a drunk Hayley didn't care and continued to wind her up. Carly then lunged over and grabbed Hayley by the hair. That's when I jumped up to separate them because Hayley was in no state to fight.

Carly, still furious and also drunk, swung her arm to hit Hayley, but Hayley managed to swerve it. As she swerved, she also stumbled, pushing me forward into Carly's path. Carly's reaction was to swing again but this time it caught me on my cheek. I immediately flinched and lifted my arm to block her next punch. In doing so, I boxed her hand away, and then she screamed. She grabbed the back of her head and stumbled over the log.

For a split-second everything went silent, then Shayla started screaming, *"You Killed Carly!"*. As she stood there screaming, I could see people in the distance running over to us. Carly looked lifeless. Her legs were folded with her knees facing to her right. Her arms were completely stretched out, with her nose pointing towards the sky and her eyes were closed. If you looked close enough, you could see a slow trickle of blood oozing from the right side of her head into the dirt, and her body was as still as a statue. This was the first time I had seen a dead body and I can't get the image out my head, nor the whispers,

"Chenade pushed her, it was revenge for the Damian Clark thing".

CHAPTER 4

SHANA'S STORY

Flipping hell, Shayla! You need to calm down!

We've had no update on Carly and my sister is losing it. The police have said that everyone who was out of their room when it happened needs to be questioned, so we were all placed in this hall. We've been in here for hours and it is proper getting to us now.

It's about 8pm and as some of the parents have started to arrive at the manor house, the interviews can finally start. But, this is so long. I don't get why they need to speak to everyone when only six of us were there. What else are people going to say? *'Chenade pushed her'* or *'I wasn't there'*. You think it would be straight forward, but the way people are chatting bare rubbish in here, I know it's going to be a long night. People are saying Carly's dead, and talking about Chenade, which I get. But what I really don't understand is why I keep hearing mine and my sisters' names in the different stories. I heard Wayne

Maxwell say that Chenade stabbed Carly with a knife that I gave her. Alaya Hoston is saying that Chenade got rushed by all three of us. It feels like the only ones not talking about us is The Pits; although they are talking about it. I just heard Marlon say to Kai that he thinks it's an accident because Chenade is too pretty to be a killer. In response, Kai asked if the theory still stands if you think Carly is prettier. Now they are comparing Chenade to *Amanda Knox*. People are losing their flipping minds in here and weirdly, it sounds like more people are worried for Chenade than upset about Carly. But the way the boydem dragged up Chenade, I still can't believe it either, proper handcuffs and everything. I knew someone would one day get Carly back for her antics, but never Chenade, not like this.

I know people are also thinking, why ain't I upset like my sister if our bestie was just killed. But the truth is, we're only friends because of her. Shayla has been obsessed with Carly since year eight when we first transferred to Thamesfield Academy. I'm not heartless, I feel bad, just not sad.

We originally moved to Thamesfield from Hackham as my dad had got a new job as an Investment Banker, paying almost triple his previous salary. With this new money, he could now afford to send us to private school and quickly had us transferred to the academy.

I hated the thought of a new school, especially a stuck-up private one. I had just started to make real friends with people who liked the same kind of things as me, then in a blink, it all changed. Shayla, on the other hand, was so excited about the thought of private school and was loving our new wealth.

I bet if it was her that had objected, we probably would not have changed schools. Mum and Dad would never admit she is the favourite, but ever since we were little Shayla has always got her way over mine. Shayla was born with an *Unconjugated Hyperbilirubinemia,* which is basically a liver condition, whereas I had no complications. But I feel like my parents have always made allowances for her because she was the 'sick child'. Her liver is fine now, thank God, she grew out of the condition, but they still treat her as though she is the needier one. I'm used to it, but it annoys me because I find myself doing the same thing, and whatever Shayla says, goes. Even when I don't agree. For example, when dad had offered to buy us new suitcases for the residential, I had wanted the purple and green one that was in the window at "JR Sports" but Shayla insisted that we got matching LV cases because she wasn't about the cheap life no more. She had managed to convince dad that it was a better choice because the 'price meant quality' and had even said that we would look like the 'poor girls' at school without them. So, dad insisted that we both have them, even though I had pleaded for the cheaper cases in JR Sports. It's like Shayla doesn't care what I think. Be it, Christmas, Birthdays, Shopping Trips, if Shayla wants it, we both get it. If Shana wants it, it is just a want. To be honest, I do wonder if she'd be this hysterical if it was me that had been pushed.

On our first day at Thamesfield, the popular Carly Rothman invited us to sit with her at lunch and Shayla was adamant that we accept the invite. I had wanted to sit on another table with the girls I had been talking to in lessons that morning, but Shayla said we needed to stick together, and that she had heard Carly was school royalty, so we were actually lucky for the invite. The girls in my lessons had differed in their opinion, they had already warned me about Carly's ways. They said although all the guys fancied her, she was a bit of a mean girl and was always starting some trouble somewhere.

As per usual, Shayla didn't care what I had to say, she liked the thought of being with the so-called "in" crowd and nothing was going to change her mind. I felt like Carly had only called us over because we were twins and had on designer bags and shoes. As she could not make us a target, it was probably safer for her to make us friends. But you can't tell Shayla this, Carly is a superhero in her eyes that can do no wrong.

This morning we woke up at 5am. I was actually looking forward to the residential. I kept thinking, for the first time in ages we would be separated from Carly and would finally get to interact with the other girls in our year. Shayla had already decided that we would wear our LV tracksuits that matched our suitcases. I hated the tracksuits, but I hated arguing with Shayla more, so I just went along with it. She wanted dad to film us on the driveway riding them around, so she could post it online. Her concept made no sense, two grown-ass people riding suitcases around is not funny. But my sister is a bit of a show-off and just wanted to make sure that those who weren't coming today, still got to see our swagger. She takes social media so seriously. Whilst eating breakfast, she gave me and dad specific instructions of how she wanted the video to look. It was like she had turned into *Rapman* on the set of *Blue Story* by the time we got on the driveway. She literally screamed at my dad for holding the phone too high, and at me, for not standing in the centre of the chalked cross she had marked on the floor. She made us reshoot the video at least 12 times before her, '*Expensive-better-quality*' suitcase broke. I couldn't stop laughing. I was thinking to myself '*Good! You should have listened to me*'.

Carly arrived at ours shortly after, about 6am. She travelled to school with us every morning. My dad had offered to pick her up on the way, but she insisted on walking over with her suitcase. My parents adore Carly, not only because Shayla does, but because Carly is serious about her school work. It's probably her only good quality other than her looks. But homework is the path to my parent's heart, and as she is always doing her homework at ours, they too, have fallen in love with her. They are always praising her parents, saying how good they have raised her, even though they have never met them, and they don't actually know what she's really like. Now I think about it, I've never even met her parents and we've definitely never been to her yard.

Once we were in the car, as per usual, we each took out our phones and scrolled our online updates. Chenade had posted a selfie captioned "*Pretty in Pink*" and I thought she looked really pretty. Her baby hairs were on point and her jumper was sick. I loved the design and the colour had complimented her chocolate-brown skin. Luckily, I didn't hit 'like' because Carly must have been looking at the same post. I heard her say in the backseat, '*Is that Chenade? She looks like a ghetto pig in pink! They need to invent a dislike button, fast!*'. Shayla proceeded by laughing as if it was the funniest joke in life. For some reason, the two hated Chenade. Carly doesn't seem to hate her as much as Shayla, but I know she really hates her bestie Taylor, or '*the pus-killer*', as she calls her.

When we first started Thamesfield, Shayla had liked a boy in the year above and did everything she could to get him to notice her, only to find out he was dating Chenade. Ever since my sister has always found a reason to hate on her, and I've always thought Carly being Carly, hates on her just to suck up to my sister. *Could you now imagine what they would say if I had liked the post?* I didn't bother to say anything to them about Carly's comment neither. I didn't want them to turn on me like they always did, so I continued to scroll. Whenever I have an opinion, I'm either too soft according to Carly or too cheap according to Shayla. I can never win with them two.

When we arrived at school, the coach was already parked on the kerb outside with the doors open, so we rushed over to make sure we had good seats. Marlon Christian-Thomas was oddly seated at the front alone, but none of us asked him where his boys were. Instead, Carly made us sit in the seats behind him. She won't admit it, but she definitely has a thing for Marlon. *Why else would you want to sit at the front of the coach?*

The journey took ages. I had to sit and listen to Carly give fashion critics as if she was the appointed fashion police, and the cheek is, everything she wears is last season or black. It only got fun when she and Hayley-Rose got into it in the toilets when we stopped. Those two often go back and forth, especially if Hayley's had a drink. But on a whole, Hayley-Rose is a cool girl, even if she is a bit wild. She's actually the one who named herself the 'Ginger Nut' because she is a proud redhead and often goes completely nuts on people, even her friends. But she always means well and is one of the only girls in my year that stands up to Carly, and for that, I really like her. I won't say what Shayla thinks of her, but it's a colour and the American slang for rubbish.

When we arrived at the Manor House, they took our phones and this BFG looking guy gave us a load of rules. Ms Strauss then allocated me to Room 7, and to be honest, I wasn't thrilled with the line-up. In reality, I didn't want to share with my sister, let alone Carly and I wasn't too keen on the other girls either. I knew Chenade didn't like us because of the phone call prank that Carly did in year 9; and everyone knows if you're looking for fun, Ashly Thomas is not the one. A lot of people think that she doesn't speak English, but I have seen her grades in English, she definitely understands. I think she's really weird or just doesn't like anyone.

With this line-up of girls, I was convinced the trip was going to be boring, so I was actually really pleased when Chenade and Carly made up in the 'stinky' room after lunch. However, I was surprised that it was Carly who had begged friends, considering the comment she had made this morning about her in the car. But I told you, she only gets on to Chenade to please my sister. Plus, Carly is like that, the girl ain't just two-faced, she's three. I know my sister wasn't pleased either, especially after she had made the issue over the beds. The way Shayla's face dropped, I actually wanted to climb down from my bunk, just to lift her jaw. I know she was vexed that Carly didn't back up her stupid comment, and instead had made friends with her enemy.

I'll be honest, I didn't give a damn how Shayla felt neither, I was looking forward to being able to talk to someone other than them. So, when Ginger Nut came through with the alcohol and we all agreed to go for a walk wearing matching outfits, I honestly thought this trip was about to get fun.

At first, it was. As we made our way to where it all happened, Hayley kept singing offbeat and mixing up the words to bashment tunes as we walked, which gave us the giggles. She had sounded more like a Russian singing a nursery rhyme than a Jamaican MC. At one point, even Ashly was laughing, especially when *The Thamesfield Pits* got on to Hayley for her singing. The boys were standing around throwing stones at the water and Kai ran over to Hayley and cuddled her because he thought she was crying. When he realised she was singing, he shook his head and said to us *'Give Nutty another drink, or take it all away, because she sounds upset'*. She tried to kick him, but he ran off too quickly and the next thing I knew she was on the floor in a seated position. I think she was too drunk to be embarrassed, but we were, so we kept it moving.

We did see them again a little later just before we crossed over the field. By this time the sky had greyed over, and it had started to feel more like the late evening than late afternoon. I only clocked the boys because Carly had pointed out that it was the first time she had seen them with Marlon today. She was saying something about them squashing a beef, but I had no idea what she was talking about, I didn't hear anything about the Pits having beef, and trust me, that news would have travelled fast in our school. It was probably Carly trying to start something, so I made sure to show my lack of interest.

Someone found a perfect spot under a tree for us to sit down. It was like nature had prepared us seats with the bushes to act as curtains from the peering eyes of teachers. Carly immediately opened the bottle of vodka, took a swig and passed it around, whilst she retold the same *dry-ass* stories she always told.

As the bottle made its way around it seemed to stop longer when it got to Hayley Rose, and the more she drank, the more she wound up Carly. She kept interrupting Carly's stories to call her *'Spiteful'*, a *'Liar'* and a *'Wussy'*. You could see Carly was getting annoyed, but she tried her best not to show it, which in turn, had encouraged Hayley to continue. She brought up the prank call that she had made to Chenade in year 9, and the #bowchallenge post, saying that she had never admitted to neither. Hayley then flipped it to Chenade and asked how she could be friends with Carly after that. Then it all happened so quickly.

Carly grabbed Hayley by the hair, then Chenade jumped up and pushed Carly who fell into the tree stump. I think Hayley might have grabbed Carly's hair at some point because, before Chenade pushed her, Carly grabbed the back of her head in pain, I didn't quite see that bit. I was watching my sister, making sure she didn't jump in. When Carly hit the ground, Shayla started screaming hysterically and people started running over. They were all saying Chenade pushed her, so it must be true, I was standing right there. How else did it happen?

CHAPTER 5

HAYLEY-ROSE'S STORY

I am going to get in so much trouble if anyone has mentioned the alcohol. I bet they say I'm partly to blame because they were drunk. My mum said if I get caught drinking again, she would send me to Norway to live with my dad. My stupid piano teacher sent an email saying I was drunk during practice last week, and that he had smelt alcohol from the moment he came in the house. She kept going on about how embarrassing it was to read the email, but I said if she was home in the evening, she wouldn't have had to read it, he could have told it to her face. In hindsight, maybe I shouldn't have said that, but I was still drunk, and it was true. My dad used to say all the time that I should say how I feel, and that the truth only offends those that don't live in theirs. It's true, but he does talk a lot of crap as well. For the past 6 months, he has promised me 11 times that he would fly back to the UK, but an excuse always comes up. His latest one is the fact that his new fiancée has had a baby and there is never a good time to leave her alone. It's a shame he didn't think like that when he left my mum.

My friends say I should be grateful because he pays my school fees and sends money every month, but my house is so boring and lonely now, how can I be grateful? Since this new baby, my mums had to work more hours, because dad can't afford to pay as much, so now she is hardly at home in the evening. I know she feels bad about it because lately I've been getting more spending money and she's willing to buy anything I ask for. And don't get me wrong, I love the money, but it doesn't make up for coming home to an empty house most days.

This morning I got up at about 5.45am. I would have overslept but mum woke me when she came in from her night shift. My head was pounding, and I felt completely hungover. I had drunk a whole bottle of vodka to myself the night before because I was so upset. My stupid ex thought that he could break up with me. He said lately I was drinking too much, and he wasn't feeling me. So, I told him that I thought he didn't drink enough, and to f' his feelings. I think I also called him a *'wasteman'*, amongst other not nice things. I know, I shouldn't have said it, but it was true, and I was still drunk.

Sometimes words come out like vomit, especially when I'm drinking. I usually regret it straight away, just like I regretted drinking so much this morning or a few hours ago, but in the moment, it feels good. I had also previously read in a post titled *'Hair of the*

Dog', that a cure for a hangover is to start drinking again. So, before I got ready this morning, I opened my suitcase and took a swig from one of the many bottles of alcohol I had packed.

The off licence up the road sells bottles of alcohol for really cheap and I get served there. I think the owner thinks I'm older because he has seen me out late on school nights with an older crowd, but regardless, he has never asked me for ID. But I never go in when his wife is working because the one time I did, she asked me for it. I had to make out like I'd left it in the car, then made my boyfriend go back and show his instead, as he was 18 with a driving licence. So now, I never go in if she's there, I know she will ask me again. However, feeling proud of my collection, I took a picture and posted it online with the caption, *"Ginger Nut got it by the 'caseload', #Literally"*. I then rushed to get ready and headed to school, I knew I was running late.

When I got there, the coach was parked outside, and Ms Strauss was waiting with her dusty clipboard. The coach looked packed and I think I was the last to board, as Ms Strauss got on behind me and then the doors closed. Once Ms Strauss had sat down, there were only two free seats left. One was next to her and the other was on the opposite side of the coach next to Marlon, so I chose the latter, as I could not risk her smelling the alcohol on my breath.

Throughout the journey, I swigged away at the cider I had opened earlier at home. I attempted to talk to

Marlon and asked why he wasn't sitting with his boys today, but he said something about getting 'travel sick' and needing to sit near the front window to see 'the horizon'. I knew he was chatting jazz because sunset has nothing to do with being sick. But I also know how to take a hint and he obviously didn't want to say what was really going on with him. He must have been upset about the beef that Carly was talking about. Plus, I hate liars, my dad is one and I know me. I would have gone off if I felt Marlon was lying to me on purpose. So, I thought to myself, sip more, talk less.

But I couldn't. Every few minutes, Carly would tap me through the gap in the seats and gesture for some of my drink. When I told her to allow it, she tried to get rude and said I was moving drunk, and that I was *'seeing things'*. She was blatantly acting up for Marlon and fronting like the drink wasn't what she was hinting for. And I knew it! When we stopped for a break, she tried to ask for some of it again, but I told her it was backwashed now and to wait until we got there, as I had a load more bottles in my suitcase. I also called her out for lying on the coach and asked why she was trying to mug me in front of Marlon, did she fancy him? Marlon must've been the trigger because she made such a scene that she nearly got us caught. Ms Strauss came in and interrogated us all, trying to find out who was making the noise and how the argument had started. I had tried to stand as far away from her as possible because I didn't want her to smell me, I was too shook to get caught. I can't remember what we all said, but I didn't, so I wasn't holding any grudges.

I got back on the coach and finished my juice. As we got closer, I became very pleased with my choice to bring so many bottles, as I hadn't seen a shop for miles. All you could see through the windows of the coach towards the end of the journey was green. It reminded me of that programme my nan used to watch, *Emmerdale.*

When we arrived at the Manor house some old guy spoke to us for about ten minutes. Ms Strauss then took our phones and stuck me in a room with a load of girls that didn't drink. After lunch, we were told we had free time until dinner, so I went and got a bottle from my case and headed straight to Room 7. I knew Carly and the Twins would want a sip.

At first, Carly was acting shook. She said we had to go for a walk as she didn't want to drink in the room. I wasn't too mad at the idea because Room 7 smelt funky. She summoned all the girls to wear black, which I didn't get, but the stupid bunch actually changed, even the quiet girl. To be fair, the twins needed to change, and Carly knew it, they looked like they had on my nan's curtains. Honestly, I don't care how much they cost, the print on their tracksuits was *'grannyish'.*

But personally, I didn't care about Carly's dress code, or what they all wore, I was happy wearing my grey velour tracksuit and having some company to drink with, despite the long-ass trek she made us do through the woods.

As usual, I provided the vibes and was making the girls laugh by singing as we walked. We saw the *'Thamefields Idiots',* a couple of times. The one with dreadlocks tried to come over and say something slick, and he was lucky I didn't have on my other crep or I would have kicked his arse. That fool made me get mud all over my trousers. I don't even know what they were doing in the bushes, they are so weird. But, 'apparently' and according to Carly, the boyband hadn't broken up, the beef was squashed, and Marlon was back with them. I don't even know what that meant, I just knew he was acting weird on the coach.

We found a decent spot, and after practically dragging the bottle out of my hand and opening it, Carly started chatting her usual rubbish to the girls, telling them a pack of lies that made her sound great. When Carly drinks she doesn't stop talking about herself. This is the norm when she's sober, but it is multiplied by ten, with a thousand lies added, when she has had a drink, and I hate liars, my dad is one. Even one of the twins had rolled their eyes a few times because she was chatting so much sh**.

Four years together at Thamefield and I still can't remember who's who with them two. I know one has a wide nose and the other has a longer face, but I couldn't tell you what name and nose belonged to whom. I just know one is a nicer person than the other. However, Carly bending the truth to make herself look good was annoying me. Seriously, I absolutely hate liars; my dad is one. So, I called her out on it and she couldn't take it.

Out of nowhere she jumps on me and starts grabbing my hair. But Chenade didn't allow it, or maybe she saw an opportunity for revenge. I don't know, but I had reminded her of what Carly did back in the day. She immediately got between us, then there was a loud slap. A second later, Carly screamed and dropped to the ground. Chenade must have slapped her then pushed her, that's why I think it's revenge.

Who stops a fight by attacking?

I didn't see all of the push as I was standing behind Chenade, I had slipped when she first jumped in because the ground was sludgy. But I saw a lot of movement and I heard everyone saying she pushed her, and Carly was laid out on the ground dead, so it must be true. You know me, I'm not one to spread a lie. Chenade pushed her, my comment about the Damian Clark prank brought back too many old feelings.

CHAPTER 6

ASHLY'S STORY

I need to say something. The amount of make-belief taking place in this hall is unbelievable. I've heard at least 5 versions of what has 'apparently' happened, and every one of them is way off. I don't know how they all missed it. This is a serious case of the *Misinformation Effect* that we learnt about in Psychology. It is when post factors, for example, things you hear or see after an event, change how you remember things.

Or it could be complete *Confabulation*, another theory we learnt about, in which your memories just fabricate and distort things without any factors. It could be both. Either way, everything I have heard in here so far has been wrong and I have to do something about it.

If you asked most people what superpower they would want, the majority would say invisibility. Well, I have been harvesting my power for the last 5 years, I am totally invisible in this school. It has its perks, but I could think of far better powers to wish for. The things I have witnessed, the conversations I have heard, you probably wouldn't believe if I told you. But people just don't see me, so I get to see things that people would only do when they feel no one is watching. I hear the comments and things people say about me, *'She doesn't speak English'*, *'She has black gums'*, *'She probably has no teeth'*. It doesn't bother me too much, because I hear the things they say about each other, even so-called friends. The comments I receive are minor in comparison, so, for me, it's worth staying quiet.

Who needs friends like these anyway?

I remember this one time in science, I had watched Shayla give Carly, Hydrochloric Acid, to pour into Tammy Acock's blazer pockets as it hung on the back of her seat. Tammy had just started dating Shayla's ex and she was not happy about it. The acid wasn't strong enough to burn Tammy but at lunchtime, I saw her outside the nurse's office with red welts all over her hand. I later heard Carly saying to Shayla, ``*Serves her right; She will now learn to keep her hands-off people's men*".

On another occasion, I had walked into the girl's toilets and Shayla and Carly were at it again. Carly was cussing about Damian Clark, saying that he had the cheek to say she wasn't his type. She said something about ending his career and was telling Shayla to post it. By the time I had got back to the classroom, I knew exactly what they had posted,

Damian Clark, #bowwowchallenge. I did not say anything to anyone about any of it, my mum always said *'Ah na everyting yuh see yuh muss talk'*.

Plus, my mum has practically sacrificed her marriage to send me to this school, I cannot afford to be distracted or in drama. She is counting on me to make something of myself and be an example to my little sister. She works so hard to provide for us both. She already has two cleaning jobs and had taken on some extra work at my uncle's restaurant, just so she could cover the cost of this trip. I was fine with not going, but when the letter stated that the trip covered topics that would contribute to our end of school grade, my mum would have sold a kidney to get me here. For her, me having strong British qualifications is important. In fact, it feels like her only goal in life sometimes, so the pressure can be a lot.

My mum is originally from Jamaica and migrated to England around 2003, with my dad and a dream. My uncle, my dad's brother, had already been living here for five years before them and had struck it lucky when he married a wealthy Irish business owner, Ms Christian. She had set him up with a Caribbean Restaurant near London's West End and my Uncle had paid for my parents to come over, in exchange for my dad's support with the business.

Back home both my parents had good jobs. My mum was a qualified midwife and my dad ran a popular trucking business, but the prospects of England appeared huge to them. Sadly, they arrived to a different reality. My mum could not get work anywhere, her nursing degree meant nothing here and she was only employable as a cleaner or in my uncle's restaurants. My dad and my uncle eventually bumped heads and the business arrangement ended after two years, not long before mum was pregnant with me.

However, my dad has always had a business brain and had invested some of his earnings in stock which had multiplied significantly over the years, so he and mum managed to stay afloat. But around 2007 England was hit with a recession and my Dad lost quite a bit of money, and that was the start of his downfall according to mum. He fell into a depression and had started to drink a lot. He and mum argued all the time, and this went on for years, but I was too young to remember. Around 2011 things in the stock market picked up and Dad reinvested some of the little savings he had left.

Things started to go well for him financially and he stopped drinking, but he still seemed unhappy. In 2013, just after my sister, Dejah, was born, he decided that he wanted to go back to Jamaica. He said England was no place for a black man and it wasn't the life he wanted. Mum did not want to leave; she was adamant that I and my sister have a British education and passport. She said they were both keys to the world and with them, we could travel and work anywhere, unlike the useless nursing degree which she had worked so hard for.

And within a week of his announcement, dad was gone. He left on good terms with mum and had agreed that he would pay for our education and a flight to Jamaica once a year. This is why my mum is so hard on me when it comes to school. She has always said that the popular and louder girls in school never usually amount to much in life because they have too many pebbles and sand grains when they should be paying closer attention to their rocks.

She has this *'Jar of Rocks'* theory that she often refers to whenever a conversation about *'priorities'* arises. In her theory, an empty jar represents life, and to fill it, you need three elements: Rocks, Pebbles, and Sand. These differ for each individual, but the principle is always the same.

Rocks represent the most important things that you could not live without like family, health and education. Pebbles represent important things, but you could live without, like books, certain foods, music and hobbies. Whilst the Sand represents the things we enjoy that are not important or essential, like fashion, TV, clubbing and boys.

For the record these are my mums' examples, music and books are rocks to me. But her theory is that to fill the jar (life) 'completely' you would need your rocks first, then pebbles, then sand. If you filled the jar in any other order, you could not fit as many of each element in, especially the rocks, which is true, I've tested it. I managed to get some different size stones from Thamesfield Park and had used a jam jar and a bit of my sister's sand.

Everything my mum said has been true and I love her theories. As you can probably tell, I love theories in general. I like to study and observe things as I hope to become a Behavioural Psychologist one day. It's literally what I do during break times, analyse everyone's behaviours. I've seen how different people are when they are in the playground in comparison to the classroom, and how different some of the girls act around my cousin.

No one even knows he's my cousin and I have kept it like that on purpose. Well, at first it was his idea. When I first moved to Thamesfield from Brixney, he had warned me not to tell anyone we were family and in the words of my mum, *'Mi nah beg nobody nuttin'*. So, if that's what he wanted, I wasn't going to beg him to change his mind. But after our family Christmas that year, we bonded so much that he wanted to let people know, but by then it was a 'no' from me, I didn't want girls to start fake-friending me to get close to him. If I was going to make friends, I wanted it to be because I was Ashly Thomas, not 'his cousin'.

He has kept to it. Even when I have heard him stick up for me, he would never say in defence - *'she's my cousin'*. So, this morning, when my uncle had to drop us both to school, we both asked to be let out on the side street so that no one saw us arrive together. I was going to take the bus originally, but when my mum felt the weight of my suitcase, she called my uncle and asked if I could get in with them.

The coach journey wasn't too bad. I sat in a window seat and spent most of the time trying to work out how far we had travelled using the *'Distance = Rate x Time'* Formula. I don't think I figured it out, but it made the journey interesting. I people-watched for a bit. I noticed Chenade and Taylor in the back seats drinking out of cans and I don't know what it is, but there is something dodgy about Taylor. I watched Hayley-Rose swallow a whole bottle of liquor right under Ms Strauss' nose. Ms Strauss must have been on a dating app or talking to a 'link' because she was so glued to her phone and smiling, she didn't even notice Hayley and her massive liquor bottle. I bet it was Mr Whitmore on the other side of the screen. She goes completely red whenever he comes into the classroom, and since his classroom got switched to her floor, she has been wearing different hairclips and lipsticks to school.

I also noticed The Pits all had on matching denim jackets, which had made me recall the conversation in the car between my uncle and cousin. Those were the hundred-pound jackets he was talking about. If I was to ever mention a hundred-pound jacket to my mum she would cuss for hours, *'Yuh kno how much mi coulda buy wit undred pound, Ashly. Mi coulda feed Yuh, Dejah, di neighbour, di cat and dem kittens fi ah whole month'*.

When it came to clothes my mum shopped between the *'Under £5'* and *'3 Items for £10'* stalls in the local market. She was always cussing out my uncle, saying that he was now an *'English Bwoy'* and that his son is a *'Silver-spooned Pickney'*.

However, she would have been proud of my uncle for this conversation, because I had actually forgotten what his Jamaican accent had sounded like until then. But on the flip side, I was disappointed with my cousin, we had already spoken a hundred times about giving in to what people think, and his reasoning for wanting the jacket was solely based on what others thought of him.

When we arrived at the manor house it reminded me of a building from a 'Goosebumps' or a 'Potter' book and the owner had reminded me of Ronald. Everyone complained about handing over their phones, and some girls were almost having meltdowns with the room allocations. I was a bit disappointed that none of the girls who go to the *'lunch library'* were in my room, but at least I had the only single bed available. Besides, it's not like I speak to any of them, it's just that us library girls have a way of communicating in silence, and I could work with that.

I know Carly thought I didn't hear her comment to the twins when I had sat on the bed, *'foreigners taking our jobs, now they're taking our beds'*. All I could think was *'Foolish gyal!'* She really doesn't bother me because I know deep down, she's got issues. Besides, that was a stupid thing to say, because although she is mixed, I'm sure she is of Caribbean decent too. Irrespective, I was willing to give her another chance because I respected her approach with Chenade. Whatever her motive, because Carly always has a motive, I appreciated the change in the atmosphere, because, at one point, I thought they were going to plot against me and her.

When Carly set her dress code, I watched all the girls go into their suitcases as I hesitantly reached into mine. They were pulling out all sorts. Makeup bags, laced underwear, crop tops and perfumes. I looked in my case, amongst my basic clothes, I had a 7-pack of full brief knickers, 4 double strapped cotton bras, a headscarf, a tub of Vaseline and Coconut oil, a roll-on and aerosol deodorant, sanitary towels even though I wasn't due on for another two weeks and a pack of multi-purpose cleaning wipes. My mum had packed my case, it was literally full of rocks. My mum also has this thing about cleaning toilet seats before you use them, hence the wipes. Everything in my suitcase matched the 25 items listed in the residential parent pack, plus a few extra hygiene cosmetics, no fancy dresses or designer trainers. I practically had to beg for her to single plait my hair in extensions, otherwise, she would have packed the ribbons too.

She has this thing about uniform and hair ribbons. Apparently, when she was at school in Jamaica it was the right school etiquette to wear ribbons. It didn't matter how much I tried to explain that she lived in England now, she didn't care, she said this is her house and in here, it's Jamaica. Luckily, she had packed a pair of black leggings and a black polo neck, so to avoid conversation, I got changed and followed them to the woods.

I remembered praying along the journey for God to make a miracle happen so that I didn't have to play dress-up with Carly for the next four days. Was Carly's death the miracle? As my mum would say *'Be careful what you wish for, cah yuh ah go get weh yuh never wan'*. I definitely had not wanted that to happen to her.

When we sat down, the liquor bottle quickly made its way around like a game of pass the parcel, but I didn't drink a sip. I could hear my mum's voice in the back of my head on how it affected my Dad. So, I was the only one that had to listen to Carly chat off her mouth with a clear mind, and I'm telling you, the girl is a storyteller. Little did she know, I had witnessed a lot of the events she was talking about, and Hayley was right, she was definitely lying in parts.

I had started looking around in desperation for a distraction, Carly's stories were slowly killing me. I had noticed in the field across from us, two shadowy figures, I think it was a couple getting it on, which is definitely not my kind of distraction. I thought I saw another person standing in the middle of the field with their arms out, but I concluded after a few minutes that it was a scarecrow, it didn't move once.

I shifted my legs away from the group to sit side-on as I still needed a new focus but didn't want to be blatant about it. I scanned around further and noticed The Pits moving around in bushes behind us. They were about 30meters away and hurling rocks into the trees, which made it look like it was raining leaves. There was another dark figure near the bushes, but I wasn't sure if it was an animal, a person or just a shadow cast from the trees opposite. I remember looking back at the boys before the fight broke out because their body language looked as if things were getting heated between them too.

When the fight did break, everyone had paid so much attention to what Chenade and Hayley were doing, that they didn't see the huge rock that hurtled in from the other side and hit Carly in the back of her head. That's why she screamed and grabbed it. She took a step back from Chenade, she wasn't pushed. Either she felt concussed and fainted or she tripped as she stepped, but I am a thousand percent certain, Chenade didn't push her. Chenade did box her hand away because Carly was ready to draw blood. If you saw the slap she gave her, you would have felt bad. But the level of force Chenade used was not even close to what was needed for Carly to fall like that.

The only thing is, I'm pretty sure I saw who threw it and I don't know if I should say anything. I can't believe that it travelled so far, and I don't think they intentionally aimed at Carly. They weren't even looking in her direction. It was definitely an accident, surely you can't go down for an accident? But the fact is, she's dead, that's why we've had no update. That means Chenade will be charged with murder because the evidence said that she pushed her and I'm literally the only one who can set her free. I've watched things like this on TV and sometimes they don't even investigate further when they think they have the murderer, so no one will ever know the truth. I've seen the statistics. One study showed at least 10000 people go to prison every year for a crime they didn't commit.

But I can hear my mum in my head, "*Not everyting yuh see, yuh must talk*" so maybe I should keep quiet, but I can also hear her saying '*it's di worse sin fi ah good person to watch bad tings happen an nah seh nutten*'.

Lord have mercy! What should I do?

We could even be dealing with a 'stone-cold' killer - Excuse the pun. But the person ran over to help Carly and had even spoken to the police at the scene. If they do know what they have done, that would be some nerve. To watch Chenade get arrested like that, you'd have to be heartless. That police officer dragged her like a rag doll as soon as everyone said she did it. But a cover-up? That is not the person I know, so, maybe one of the others clocked and now they are all conspiring.

This is a lot to comprehend. Apparently, things have always been awkward between my mum and my uncle since it went left with my Dad and the restaurant. If I say something, it could destroy my family for good. I would be the girl who sent her cousin to jail. Maybe I should tell him what I know first because if I saw, maybe someone else out there saw and that would force him to confess. I did see that couple near the field and it looked like someone might have been in the bushes. Yes, that's exactly what I'm going to do. I'll call him over and we can stand outside the hall and talk, none of the others should hear this for now.

But he's sitting with so many people, how am I going to get his attention without all the heads turning, I can't scream out his name. Maybe I should just walk over there.

Okay, I'm walking.

Now watch the whole room stop and stare,

'Marlon, can I talk to you outside?'

CHAPTER 7

MARLON'S STORY

My heart nearly flipped out my chest when my cousin called my name in the hall. I knew something serious was up because Ashly has never approached me in school, let alone in front of half the year group. As serious as I thought things were, I had no idea just how serious it actually was. I practically had to beg Mr Adinbola, the male supervisor, to use his phone to call my mum. He said all parents had already been notified and would be here shortly, but hearing what Ashly told me, I couldn't wait, I needed to speak to her straight away.

I made a whole lie about losing my inhaler in the commotion and needing her to bring a spare one. The minute I mentioned it was medical, he snuck me his mobile. I briefed mum on what had happened and swore that it was an accident, but she told me that dad had said to keep quiet until my solicitor got here. I could hear him cursing in the background. He had opinions on how police treated young black men, and although I was only half black, he has always said, in the eyes of most I am a black man first and will be treated and trialled as such.

He ain't lying, I have been stopped and searched bare times in the last few years, yet my best friend Chris who is white, has only ever been stopped once, and it was because he was with me. They would always suspect me of drug-dealing or theft because, 'apparently', I fit the profile of their suspect. It's funny because Kai has been stopped more times than me in the same area, for the same reason, yet we look totally different, he is a lot darker-skinned than I am and has dreadlocks. So, it does make you wonder what the hell the original suspect looked like.

One time, Callum Burgess, Timmy Shaw and Andrew Burke, 3 white guys, had stolen eggs from a corner shop near the school and egged several houses on the same street. That day, Kai, Chris and I had been walking back from the library when a police officer grabbed me by the back of my blazer and tried to drag me down. I shoved his arm away, because at the time I didn't know it was an officer, and he drew his baton. He then radioed for back up saying an officer had been assaulted by one of the suspected robbers. Within seconds there were about 12 officers at the scene and I had my face slammed to the ground. When we got to the station and they found out we were minors, and that my mum was white, they all started to act differently. Can you believe they had accused us of stealing the eggs and egging the doors? We were two black kids and a white kid in school uniform, that they happened to mistake for three white boys, because 'apparently' our clothing matched the description. Do you know how many people, closer fitting their descriptions, left the library that day in our uniform, that didn't end up with floor burns on their faces? I won't force you to any conclusions, but all I'm saying is, as a black man, I am not confessing to a possible murder without a lawyer. Especially when it was a genuine accident. Besides, that officer with the dog looks like the same officer that stopped me last week, and he was a proper prick. And the big one that arrested Chenade, Bruv! He was on a 'mad ting'.

I'm not going back into the hall either, I'll wait out here for the solicitor. Mum said a local colleague from the firm was on route, so he should arrive soon. I also don't want to hear anyone's 'Ashly' questions right now, I saw the faces when she called my name, of course, they are going to ask questions. I feel bad, but I'd rather let Ashly face them alone. That girl is a G, she is built differently to me.

She is built differently to most people in this school. I never admitted it, but in year 7, I was embarrassed to tell people she was my cousin. She used to wear her hair in 6 puffy bunches with these massive white ribbons around them. From a distance, she looked like she had a load of tissue stuck on her head. Her square front shoes didn't help either, they had looked three sizes too big and had a weird fur bit on the side. She had looked like an old maid with clown feet. But that was then.

That Christmas a load of my dad's family had come over from Jamaica for the holidays and I got to spend time with Ashly. As I said, that girl is a G, she has way more brains and substance than most of the girls at Thamesfield. However, by then she was happy with her position at school and this time, she didn't want no one to know we were cousins. She said she didn't want any attention or girls to beg friends with her, as this was just after the talent show and everyone in school knew my face. I had to respect her wishes.

I got up mad early today to come here. To be honest, I wasn't really on coming, but I had spoken to Ashly two nights ago and she had motivated me. She kept hinting that Chenade liked me and as I had been feeling her for time, this would be a perfect opportunity to move to her.

I like girls like Chenade, she's pretty, smart and so down to earth, unlike a lot of these girls who have been trying it lately. I'm not too sure about her bredrin though, she's weird.

I had been looking forward to the Year 11 residential since year 7. The Pits and I were going to get my dad's chauffeur to take us instead of getting on the coach. The plan was to pull up at the manor house five minutes after the coach, so when everyone was outside gathering their luggage we would arrive and make a scene. We had planned the music for our entrance and were going to wear matching customized denim jackets. That was before my Dad decided to put in for another restaurant and it changed everything.

All of a sudden, he's telling me that I needed to grow-up and start saving if I wanted these things. He went on a rant about when he grew up and how far he had to walk to school every day. I told him I didn't get it and had asked why a rich man would invest in something that made him so broke that he could no longer afford to buy his son a jacket? He went ballistic. Thank god for my mum, because I think he wanted to kill me that day. He took all my clothes and threw them in the pool. He cussed for about an hour straight. My dad literally turned from Santan Dave to Bounty Killer. He kept saying, *'I can't believe me come ah England fi mek dunce'* and told me I needed to go study more books and I should forget chauffeurs and denim. He even asked my mum if they are paying the school to lie, because my question could not come from someone who gets straight A's.

He just didn't get it and I knew my boys wouldn't either. How could I say I'm now broke? I would have gone from 'topboy' to 'flopboy'. So, I told them that my Jacket got delayed in New York with the designers. I suggested that we wear something different, but they weren't on it. They were adamant I get something new. They kept saying I was already a flop because they had to get the coach now, so the least I could do was buy another denim jacket. It wasn't even worth asking my dad, so I just talked myself out of going.

That was until Ashly talked me back into it. She said I was shallow, especially when she found out we were only wearing the jackets for the journey. After hearing what was in her suitcase, I realised I was a bit shallow, but I couldn't get depth overnight, so she helped me come up with a diversion, a reason to not make the journey with the boys. I knew they wouldn't want to sit at the front, so the 'travel-sick' story was perfect. I told them that my Dad was dropping me straight to the coach because my suitcase was too heavy, and as long as I left it until after they had sat down before I got on the coach, we wouldn't be seen together until after we arrived. I told you, Ashly is a G.

The journey was long. I had that dumb chick Carly and her friends sitting behind me, and the smell of a pub to my left. Carly and the louder twin were being so annoying, and mix-up. All they did was talk about other girls the entire journey like they were trying to prove to each other how much better they were. Don't get it twisted, I'm not blind, Carly is peng, but she's an idiot. Jake used to fancy her back in the day, and she used to mug him for it. Everyone knew he wasn't her type, but she used to lead him on as a joke; he had wanted it to be true so badly, that he started to believe it was. He was literally linking her in his head. No matter how much me and the Pits tried to show him he was being mugged off, he wouldn't have it, and in turn, called us '*hettas*'. That's how the word '*haters*' sounded in his accent. You see, Jake has only lived in England for 5 and a half years. When I first met him at induction, he was what we called a "*freshie*", so some of his social queues when it came to these '*Thamesfield gyallies*' weren't as sharp as the mandem. Whenever she saw him at 'The Chick-in Shack' she would purposely wait for him to be at the front of the queue before acknowledging him. She would always use the same deadline to finesse a meal. Whenever he said her name it sounded like '*Curly*' instead of Carly, and she would always giggle, fix his tie and say, '*Curly Fries for Curly's thighs*'. It sounds innocent on paper, but her tone and the mimicking of his Congolese accent was a piss-take. She knew exactly what she was doing every time she fixed his tie. A blind man could see how gassed he would get when she spoke to him, let alone touched near his neck. But her manipulation worked because she always ended up with a free meal and he was the meal ticket. She would never speak to him no other time. She literally did this for a whole term, until Jake decided he was going to make an actual move on her.

It was the usual lunch routine and Jake was at the front of the queue. Like a notification, Carly popped up, touched his tie, collected her free meal and headed out the door. This time, Jake got his meal to take-away and scurried behind to catch her up, trying not to make it obvious to those inside the shop of what his intentions were. But when he popped his head around the door frame to see how far she had got; she was standing right outside, talking to a guy from the year above.

"Told you I got it like that. In the Shack, number 2 is my favourite meal and free is my favourite price".

That is what she had said, as she leant forward and planted a kiss on the guy's lips. She then popped a curly fry into his mouth, before the two turned and walked off together. Jake was livid and in his best British accent, loud enough for her to hear, he called her a *'Dotty Skunk!'*, translated as 'dirty skank'. He had finally realised she was not flirting with him; she was finessing him.

I can't lie, before this, I would have said, in the words of my dad, that *'she deserves to get a lick in her head with a big stone, it might soften her heart'*, but I would never wish for this or intentionally harm a female. I don't even know how the stone travelled that far and hit her that hard. It was the size of a pebble and I was aiming into the tree. But Kai was annoying me at the time, so I was distracted. He is always trying to get on to me and has been doing so since we had linked back up. He is like my brother from another mother, I can't lie, but sometimes, the constant *'light-skin vs dark-skin boy'* jokes can be too much. When we were at the bushes, we were doing our usual back and forth, he kept calling me *'Bart Simpson',* about my skin tone, and I was calling him *'The Black Medusa'* about his and his dreads. That was our normal banter. But what irritated me the most today was him continuously saying that light-skins guys were moist and using the examples of me sitting at the front of the coach to prove it; He didn't know how much balls it took to sit at the front.

So, when I dashed the stone, I was actually in my feelings. Although, maybe man is stronger than I thought, because it didn't feel like I threw it that far. Or could Ashly be over exaggerating? The stone wasn't as big as she described. *Nah*! She saw me throw it, and to be fair, that girl is never wrong about things. So, it probably is true, man is kind of *hench*!

Finally!

I think this is my solicitor walking in. I recognise the logo on his lanyard from the business card on my dad's desk. It has to be him, I just heard him say my name and ask one of the workers for a private room to use. He has been directed to the red door opposite the entrance and Mr Adinbola is now pointing over in my direction, ushering me to come over. I slowly walk into the room and sit down, but as soon as the red door closes, my tears break free. I try but I can't stop them.

The room started to spin, and it felt like I couldn't breathe. I had a vision of being locked in a cell and it frightened me. My breathing went so mad that I thought I was having an asthma attack. I was so nervous to talk to the solicitor who was standing behind the tucked in chair at the table, stretched over his laptop when I walked in. He just looked like another fed to me. Without eye contact, he said hello and told me to sit down. But when I didn't respond, he walked around the table, put his hand on my shoulder and told me to *calm down*, which seemed to make the tears build up even faster. Halting the tears with my sleeve, I looked up at him with curiosity.

"Did you say - Calm down? You do know I have just killed someone?"

He smirked, then pulled the chair that was in front of his laptop closer to mine and sat down. Once again, he told me to *'calm down'*, but this time he also added, *'no one is dead!'*.

I literally cried a few tears of relief. He went on to say that Carly is alive, and her condition is considered stable, but she is unconscious because they have kept her sedated. Apparently, her blood alcohol levels are too high for them to wake her, as they cannot be sure how the alcohol will affect her behaviour. He said before I confess to anything, he needed me to tell him exactly what had happened, so he could advise me best on what to tell the police.

When I had finished explaining everything that I had remembered, along with what Ashly had told me, he laughed. His laugh was so patronising. It actually pissed me off because this was my life on the line and he was taking it for a joke. When he saw I did not smile, he had the cheek to tell me to 'calm down' again. He said from my version of events and the information in the police report, there was no way the stone I threw was the one that caused the injury. Although hitting the ground had knocked her out, the gash on the back of her head was caused by something that had a sharp or jagged edge, like the large, chipped stone found at the crime scene. The smooth pebble stones that could be found near the water, that I had described, could not have caused it.

However, he did say that Ashly was partly right in the description of the rock and the fact that it was thrown, but the questions were, who did it and why?

CHAPTER 8

I DIDN'T MEAN IT

I've probably done a hundred laps around this dorm room, but I just can't keep still. I feel like I can't breathe, and I can't stop thinking. I can't believe I have killed somebody! I can't believe I killed Carly!

I'm waiting for the police to knock on this door at any minute, looking for me, because I know Ashly saw me in the bushes. She looked right at me. But the way Shayla screamed, it had made me panic and I knew I had messed up big time, so I ran. When I saw the police and ambulance arrive through the window, I knew it was bad. I just had no idea how bad, until I had overheard a few girls as they walked past the room door. They were saying that Carly was dead and that they had arrested Chenade for it. I can't let Chenade take the wrap, but I can't go to prison. Not for life. I just need a bit more time to think of a plan. I need my Dad, he would understand. I swear, I didn't mean it, I just wanted her to stop. I really didn't mean to kill her.

It's just, she's done it to me before, so what kind of idiot would I be to make the same mistake twice? I couldn't handle losing another best friend, not to her. I've known Carly since primary school and at one point in history, she was kind of alright. I mean, we were never friends, but she never bothered me or got in my way. That was until the middle of year 6. I can't remember why, but she had left the school for a few months and when she returned it was like she had changed for the worse. It's like she had turned evil, and wanted to ruin people's lives, well, mine at least.

I remember one weekend my aunty had done my hair in 'chiney bumps', like the girl from her favourite childhood group, TLC. I absolutely loved it, and so did my dad, he said it made me look like an African-doll. The following Monday I waited for my best friend Jodie at the school gates, excited to show off my new hairdo. Since we were allowed to walk to school on our own, we had made a pact that whoever got to school first, would then wait for the other at the entrance and we would always walk into the playground together. Regarding my hair, Jodie said she loved it.

On that same Monday afternoon, our teacher Ms Griffiths had to leave school early for a personal emergency and our class was split into groups of six and were allocated to other classrooms. Carly and Jodie were put in the same group and must have bonded in their session because during the last break time that day, they played together. I wasn't too upset, because they had let me watch them play but I had wished they would have spoken to me more. However, Jodie smiled at me twice, so I knew things were okay. But the next morning I waited at the school gates for Jodie and she didn't show up. I really thought something bad had happened to her. When the bell rang, and I finally walked into the playground, there she was, with Carly, laughing and joking whilst I had been standing outside waiting. To make it worse, when I went over to her and asked why she didn't wait for me, she told me to *'chillout spidy'*, referring to my hair. Then they looked at each other and burst into laughter. As I turned and walked away, thinking Jodie would call me back, I heard Carly say, *"I was meant to say the spidy joke"*, followed by even more laughter. That moment literally broke me, and I blame Carly, Jodie would never have made a joke like that before. I remember going to the toilets and screaming in rage. I ripped up every bit of toilet paper in there and had used the tip of my compass to scratch the cubicle door. I kept imagining it was Carly's face. That evening I told my mum what had happened and asked her to take out the chiney bumps. I thought she was going to help me get Jodie back, but she was angry with me. She didn't care about what Carly and Jodie did, all she went on about was me wasting my aunt's time and her money. She said if I was more like them, she wouldn't be here playing hairdresser when her business is wine bars, and that's when it clicked, I needed to be more like them. Especially if it would make my mum happy and get Jodie back.

My mum is always irritable when it comes to me. The only time she isn't, is when my friends are over, so that is why I always try to be more like my friends. When I try to be me, no matter how hard I try, I am always a waste of her time. I really look up to my mum, she has built 3 businesses by herself, so her advice is golden. That is why I have always tried to do what she has said to me and be more like them. That's why I hate Carly. Just as I was being more like Jodie, she took her away. I always hoped one day I would get to the school gates and Jodie would be there waiting, but she never was and that was Carly's fault. Things would have been different between me and my mum if I had just been more like Jodie or got rid of Carly sooner.

So, when I got to Room 7 after lunch, to go and check up on my 'now' best friend, whom my mum adores, and I saw her laughing and joking with Carly, in matching outfits and not missing me at all. Suddenly, all my old fears started flooding back and I felt like I was losing my best friend all over again. Matching outfits were our thing, that's how we had arrived this morning.

Since year 7 we have been best friends and she means everything to me. My mum loves her and our friendship, which is why she's so important to me. She has brought me and mum closer. We do everything the same and even have matching bedrooms, well, she had it decorated first. I remember she posted a picture online of her lying on her bed, and I image-searched the bedsheets and wallpaper so that I could get them. But that's how close we are, we even sleep the same way. And dress the same. She had left her *nextday.com* account logged in on my laptop, I'm sure she did it on purpose for me to check her order history. Regardless, if I see her buy something, I literally go and get it, but in a different colour, of course. It's not like I'm trying to be her, just 'more like'. But I do need to get her *dressed.com* account details because she's been buying from there lately and not telling me, which has really been stressing me out.

But that's another reason I hate Carly, she goes around telling people that I am a copycat because of how I dressed when we were in primary school in comparison to now. She tells people that I am stealing my besties swag because I don't have 'taste' on my own. She's just mad that Shayla has a twin and me and my bestie are like twins, and no one wants to join her in her stupid *'Everyday black'* look. She even told people that I killed her cat. I didn't kill it, but I did take it to the cat shelter, to protect it from her because I love cats. I don't kill animals, what happened to the rabbit was an accident. At the shelter, I told the worker that the cat was mine, but I was having a new baby sister and my mum said we couldn't keep it. With a few tears and smiles, no one asked any questions and took the cat to safety and gave me the collar as a keepsake. Can you believe on top of the 'cat killing story', she even tried to tell people I used to stalk her because she saw me near her house a few times? But I wasn't stalking her, I was checking to see if Jodie was there, I needed to make sure she was okay. That's what you do when you love someone, you protect them. If only you knew all the things she has done to me and what I've had to deal with, then you would understand. That's why tonight had to happen, she needed to be stopped before she hurt someone again. Carly had hurt her before, about 2 years ago, and I did nothing. So tonight, I had to do something, I had to protect my friend. That's what I'm going to tell the police, it wasn't murder, it was self-defence, kind of.

When I got to room 7 and saw the girls walking down the corridor laughing and joking, I followed them out. I needed to be certain that I was being betrayed before I said anything. I watched them giggle through the woods, with Hayley's drunk-ass making a bag of noise. It's probably why none of them heard me. I saw them flirting with the Pits. They were acting so thirsty, play-fighting and over-laughing with them. The worst thing is, the boys ain't even that peng. When they sat down on the logs, I hid in the bushes, just to the right of where the boys were throwing stones.

I couldn't get a clear sight and was about to walk away when I remembered I had brought the *"BackUp Phone"*. I always knew it would come in handy. I started the backup phone 2 years ago after my mobile crashed and I had to do a factory reset. I lost all my photos and messages, meaning all the memories of our friendship up until that point were gone. I had things like the photos from our first lunch at the "Chick-in Shack" on our year 6 induction day. I had walked in and she was sitting alone on a stool at the 'eat-in' counter. Her legs dangled under and her body faced the door, so she had her back towards me. I couldn't stop staring, she had reminded me so much of Jodie. She was eating a number 2 meal and scrolling online, that's how I knew she was on *Socials*. She turned around and smiled at me, and whilst I waited for my meal, a number 2 of course, I took some shots of us together. I made it look like I was taking selfies, but it was actually 'our' first photo shoot. We weren't friends then, but I did send her a friend request online the day after, and she accepted, so, she actually wanted to be my friend too. Throughout the summer holiday, I kept an eye on her page and learnt about her life and family, but I needed a way to get her to be my friend offline. I started going to the ANCC on a Sunday because her dad owned it and that's where our friendship started. I knew she loved music, so I would bring her free merchandise that my dad would get from work, and it got her attention. On the first day of year 7, I was the only person she knew, so we immediately made a pact to stick together. A bit like mine and Jodie's pact, only, she is a much more loyal friend. We became inseparable, taking turns to stay over at each other's houses on alternate nights.

[Deep Breath]

Thinking about the old phone is making my blood boil and I can feel that rage again. I even had the videos from our first sleepover on there. We had both slept in pink silk pyjamas. She sleeps with one hand clamped between her thighs and the other, under her right cheek and has a light and subtle snore which sounds so cute. I didn't actually notice it at first, but when I played the video back a few times, you could faintly hear it. I proper miss that video. But something in my gut said to bring the phone, and I'm glad I did. Usually, I keep it in the *'Friendship'* box, under my bed, so no one knows about it. Inside are so many memories of the friendships that I have had. I've got a blue diamante cat collar, a lid from the bottle of juice that I had once shared, Letishna's purple headband, silk pyjamas and a notebook. I really do take care of my things and my friends. I've even kept the rabbit foot as a reminder of Jodie, and for luck.

I reached under my top and retrieved the phone that was wedged between my bra strap and chest bone and switched it to camera mode. I needed to use the zoom function to get a better look at what was going on. Carly was in the middle looking as if she was holding a church sermon. The girls were so fixated on her that you would have thought they were witnessing the second coming of Christ.

Ashly was the only one who looked away and that's when I think she saw me. I was going to leave at that point but then Chenade stood up, and Carly got up in her face. I knew Hayley would be too drunk to defend her, Ashly just wouldn't do anything, and the minions would probably try to jump in, so I had no choice, I had to save her. I couldn't run over, as to how would I explain why I was there? Plus, it would have taken too long. I could feel the rage building inside. So, I looked down and saw a grey stone laying in the dirt in front of me. It was about the size of a golf ball but was shaped a bit like a rugby ball. It was quite chipped and one of the sides had a flat edge. I threw it at Carly's direction and seconds later she dropped to the ground. For a split second, I was so happy that I had saved Chenade, but the way Shayla screamed, and everyone looked down, I panicked and ran.

I have to tell Ms Strauss everything. I have to save Chenade, again. As I walked out the door to the bottom of the corridor, I could feel my heart thumping through my chest, and my mouth drying up. I swallowed deep, trying to use my spit to make moisture, but it made it worse and my mouth became sticky. Damn, if I feel like this, imagine how Chenade must be feeling? She must be so scared.

As soon as I pulled the double doors to the reception and waiting area, I saw Ms Strauss with her clipboard in hand, standing near the entrance to the hall. I saw Marlon and Ashly standing next to some guy in a business suit and also noticed that quite a few police officers were hanging around. One was stationed near the fire exit and was holding the lead of a police dog, it was quite surreal, it no longer felt like the same place that we had eaten our lunch earlier. I saw one of the twins crying hysterically, which made me feel even more guilt. Imagine losing your best friend like that, imagine that was my bestie, I couldn't even stomach the thought. I immediately walked over to Ms Strauss and whispered; I know the truth.

Looking concerned, she pulled me to a side room and told me to explain exactly what I meant. As soon as I mentioned the rock, she stopped me. She said she needed to get someone and left the room. She returned with a uniformed officer and a little short lady in casual clothes. She looked a bit like an unfit PE teacher, but apparently, she was part of child services and had to be present. They explained that despite being 15, I could be questioned and charged on the spot, for any crimes they felt were committed, but as this was a school trip, Ms Strauss would act as a witness to ensure I was being handled appropriately. My parents had signed the trip's consent for her to act as my legal guardian whilst we were away. To be fair, she'd play a better 'stand-in mum' than my mother, at least she has a bit more patience. I could imagine my mum right now,

"Why you got these people wasting my time? - I could have called*! - Do you know how much money I'm missing out on being here?"*

I have asked my dad in the past if mum regrets having me. He said no. He said that mum doesn't hate me, she just thinks I waste her time a lot and she hates that, but I know he's lying, she does regret it. Just before my mum got pregnant with me, she was studying for her 'Masters' in Fermentation Science. My grandparents, originally from Angola, owned a large vineyard in Italy which had been in the family for hundreds of years. It was a gift to my great great great great great grandfather from his masters, after slavery was abolished. The rumour was that my grandfather was actually the master's son because his skin was so fair, and the gift was almost an admission of his guilt. My mum always said my fair skin and natural red hair was a throwback from his genes. But the vineyard was something that had provided my family with generational wealth and was to be passed on to my mum, the eldest child, once she had graduated. After meeting my dad at uni, she ended up falling pregnant with me. This was just before her final year. Her pregnancy was so bad that she was unable to complete her studies, and for several years my grandparents resented her. They felt she had failed and shamed them. With seven kids, their only daughter was pregnant out of wedlock and 'uneducated' in their eyes. For a long time, they felt they had raised a 'whore' and gave the vineyard to my uncle. I've never really got to know mums' side of the family, and my dad, like me, is an only child, so it has always been just us three. He agreed to be a house-husband to allow her to pursue a career, as she didn't like the thought of hiring a nanny and having another woman in the home; nor did she see herself as a 'stay at home' mum. Despite not going back to finish her degree, she was still very determined to create her own wealth. Turn lemons to lemonade and squashed grapes to wine are mum's motto. That attitude has already got her three wine bars at the age of 35. So, you see, I have to learn to get on with things and be like 'them', that is what she said about the chiney bumps situation, I should have been more like Carly and Jodie. Especially after messing up her degree and vineyard, I can't be wasting more of her time. I just have to face this on my own, or at least until my dad gets here.

After I was read my rights, the PE lady started to question me about my health, drugs and alcohol, before asking me to explain what I knew. I began telling my side of the story. I told them all about Carly's antics, the rumours she was spreading about me and all the friends she had stolen in the past. I explained how angry I felt when I saw them laughing outside the room and how it had reminded me of her and Jodie on the bench all them years ago. I told them how I zoomed in and saw first-hand that Carly had launched the attack on the other girls, which explained why what I did was self-defence. I was protecting my bestie. Although I couldn't be charged for anything to do with Carly, as far as I'm concerned that was self-defence, I still felt anxious. The way the adults in the room were looking at me and each other, I knew that I had messed up by mentioning the phone. But I had to ask what would happen to it, my biggest fear was losing our memories again. The officer had the cheek to say that the phone was the least of my worries, but I tried to explain that it was in fact, my biggest. He was so dismissive and continued to make eye gestures to the other adults in the room. I was getting that feeling again like I was about to lose my friend, that feeling of rage was building inside. So, to calm me down, I rocked back and forth in the seat and repeated,

Self-defence is not a crime! I was only protecting what was mine!

The PE lady looked at Ms Strauss, then at me, and as if she had expected me to change my answer, she again asked if I had any history of mental health. She reckoned I needed to talk to somebody or at least be evaluated. But maybe she was right, I did need to talk to somebody, my dad and a solicitor, perhaps? They would sort out the phone issue. Besides, I've already evaluated the situation, it was self-defence, she deserved it, and if that's all I get for killing Carly, then I would kill her again. The officer then grabbed my arm and proceeded to say:

Taylor Henry, I am arresting you for the attempted murder of Carly Rothman. You do not have to say anything, but it may harm your defence if you do not mention...

Wait! Wait a minute! She's alive?

...something you later rely on in court. Anything you do say may be given in evidence!

CHAPTER 9

CARLY'S STORY

Where am I and how did I get here? The last thing I remember is someone screaming. Why do I have all these tubes in my nose and …. Aaargh! My head is banging, I can't even move it. From the signs and these machines, I'm guessing I'm in a hospital. First of all; Why the hell is Adrianne sitting over there in the chair and where the hell is Anthony? Probably his usual '10 minutes away'.

If this was anyone else I know that was laying here, they would have had their entire family waiting at the end of their bed, but not me. No! I get Adrianne, my brothers 'eediat' girlfriend and her fake Loui bag. It's like, do I have to be a *'20 bag of weed'* or a bottle of vodka to get any of my family here?

If Adrianne is here, Anthony knows I'm here, of course, he definitely sent her. But as for my mum, good luck trying to find her. She left out Sunday night in her fur coat, so it's unlikely that she will emerge until at least Wednesday. The fur coat is always a sign that she's off on one, and if she leaves out in the leather jacket, it means she's found a 'new boyfriend'. Either one, she's usually back after 3 days, with a couple of cans of beer, a bottle of brandy and all the reasons why I ruined her life. That'll last for a few days and then she's off again, different jacket same cycle. She probably doesn't even know I'm here; Anthony paid the fees and signed the consent forms. As unreliable as Anthony is, if it wasn't for him, I'd probably starve. In his own little way, he looks out for me, if he's not high or in jail, that is.

He used to come to the house every day, but the last time he came around, he and mum had a massive argument. He was asking her for his birth certificate and some other info so that he could apply for his passport, but mum was in a state and couldn't find it. She tipped the house upside down looking for it, but when Anthony saw the stack of unopened red letters that she pulled from under the sofa he lost it. He called her a *'drunk slag'* and started to question where all the money that dad had sent her had gone because she obviously wasn't using it to be a mum to me. Who told him to say that? The word 'Dad' is a trigger for mum. Like a shot put, she picked up the ashtray and threw it in his direction and it smashed to pieces, he then called her a *'madwoman'* and laughed as he turned to leave. She grabbed a piece of the broken ashtray and chased him through to the front door. She called him a *'Drug Dealer'* and told him to never come back, and he hasn't.

She laid into me that evening, saying that if she finds out that I've taken money from him, she's kicking me out because she doesn't want a '*Drug Mule'* in her house. Now, to avoid drama, he doesn't come anywhere near the house, but he sends a paid take away to the block every night unless I'm at the twins. He usually sends me a text when the driver is downstairs so that mum doesn't see; and every Monday at 8.15am, without fail, his worker meets me at the bottom of my block to give me £15 for the week unless he's locked up and not making money.

I remember the time he went to jail for a driving ban. My mum was at her worst, and I didn't have a penny for 3 months. If it wasn't for Jake, I wasn't eating lunch. I felt so bad for leading him on because he is such a sweet guy, but I was hungry, and my dickhead boyfriend at the time was always asking me for money, so he couldn't afford to buy me lunch. And the way Shayla is always cussing broke people, I could never ask the twins.

My dad is about, somewhere. He pays for my school and sends money that I never see every month. Most birthdays he will visit with my snobby step-sister and it is always awkward, but other than that, I don't see him. Him and my mum clash, big time. He said he can't stand to be around her, even more so since she started drinking and that he can't take the constant headache from her whenever he has me around him. Either way, I am not expecting him to be here.

They first separated towards the end of year 5 in primary school and that summer they shared custody of my brother and me. We spent alternate weeks with each of them. My dad was living in his then girlfriend's house, and for a long time, my mum was unaware. When she found out that's where we were staying, she went ballistic and demanded he brings us back to the house. When we pulled up, she ran out and smashed the driver side window, and that was the first time that I had ever smelt alcohol on her or seen her drunk. I had never seen her act like that before neither, it was literally the day she changed.

She began to drink every day after that and resented me and my brother for not telling her about Dad's girlfriend. She said we were ungrateful, disrespectful and that we had betrayed her. It's like she never forgave us and just stopped being a mum. For the first weeks of the new term, I didn't even go to school. Mum was no longer getting up before 11am and she hadn't washed any of our clothes for weeks. It was only after the lady from child services came to the house that she said to us, *"I don't give a damn if they took you away, but If you don't want to go, sort yourselves out"*.

And we have ever since. I learnt from young, I am the only person who is really looking out for Carly. Everyone else has someone else, but as for me, I have myself and I; and Anthony sometimes.

That's why I go hard and take no crap from the mandem, I am not trying to be that broken woman like my mum. A little bit of hurt and she falls apart, that will never be me. I'm too smart for that. I use guys, they don't use me.

I want to be rich, like Shayla and Shana's parents, the twins have everything and more, not one worry in life. They really are the *'Twinibadians'*. I've never been to their house and the Wi-Fi was cut off, or the fridge is empty or them not know where their parents were. They have a whole separate room in their house just to study, and spare laptops. I haven't even got Wi-Fi, let alone a laptop. That's why I do most of my homework at theirs. How do I tell them I'm going to the library to use the internet because my Wi-Fi got cut off years ago? For a short while I had figured out the default password to my neighbours' router, but he eventually clocked on. The old man had stopped me one evening in the block and said he knew I was using it, and he would be willing to do a favour for a favour, that's if I wanted the new password. He kept complimenting my figure and saying I reminded him of a black Britney Spears in my uniform. The man was older than my dad and I had no idea who this Britney Girl was. I always thought the lady who sang, *I will always love you,* was black, and my mum loved her. But what I did know was, he was dodgy, and the internet was not worth that much to me, I didn't need and wasn't doing any favours. I could go to the twins like I had been doing for the past few years. There, I get to sit in luxury and use the Wi-Fi free of charge. This is why I could never let them come to my house, how would I explain the bedsheet that we use as a curtain or the holes in the kitchen and bedroom doors or why there is a small TV on a chest of drawers in the living room? I just couldn't.

So, Adrianne has just told me my brother is outside getting an update from an officer, but from what she was told when she first arrived, a girl called Chenade had been arrested for attacking me. I know I hit my head but that doesn't even sound right. I remembered who I was with, and it doesn't make sense. The last thing I remember was, I was arguing with Hayley and I dashed her to the ground, Chenade had nothing to do with it. But if she had jumped in, the twins would have dealt with her. Besides, I'm sure we squashed our beef. See, I told you, Adrianne is an eediat, she can see I've licked-up my head and the first thing she does is chat some foolishness. *Where the hell is my brother?*

But no way would 'perfect' Chenade do that. She doesn't do anything wrong, apart from hanging around with Taylor. Other than that, everything about her is just so right. She hardly wears any make-up or weave, and every boy I have ever liked at Thamesfield seems to fancy her. No matter what she wears, she looks good. No matter what she says, she sounds good. You humiliate her, she becomes a hero. Teachers love her, boys love her, girls love her, and she doesn't even do anything.

I hated that I went along with Shayla's prank call idea, but I needed to keep my friend happy. Since the Twins have been around, things have felt a bit better, it's like I get to be part of a family for a few hours a day. I bet Chenade has a loving family, so she wouldn't get it. I bet her mum still makes her bed, and her dad says that she's beautiful and I bet they buy her whatever she wants, she always has new school bags and shoes. She's probably got family holidays booked and shopping sprees planned, it even sounds exciting.

In my boring life, the closest thing to a shopping spree that I can remember is the pile of old clothes that my cousin says I can take if I want. That's why I always buy black, no one can really tell if you wear the same thing twice or if they're cheap. I also found out online, that if you put a piece of charcoal in the washing machine with the clothes, it stops them looking faded, so I can make things last even longer. I'm always stealing charcoal from the art room, but I would never actually 'steal-steal', I'm not a thief like that. Broke people still have morals. I actually liked Chenade's jumper this morning as well, but I know Shayla, if she thinks I like pink then she will start sending me links to clothes online and telling me to come shopping with her, and I just can't take the embarrassment. I can't even afford the carrier bags in the type of places they shop.

It hasn't always been like this, there was a point when I had a good life. Two parents and a big house. It seems like so long ago, but I can still remember. My mum used to be a director of a hedge fund company. She was always suited and booted. She went to the hairdressers twice a week and always took us out to eat. Marlon's dad's restaurant was our favourite, *The Taste of Yard,* it was the only place that my dad didn't complain about the food. He and Mr Thomas were always going back and forth about whose island was better, St Lucia or Jamaica, and it always ended in a mini soca vs dancehall dance-off. I used to get so embarrassed to see my dad move his hips and thrust forward like he was making love to the air, and would literally die when my mum got involved, she dances like she's having seizures. My dad's sister used to say she could whine good for a white lady, but they were lying.

They were the good old days. The days when Anthony used to be obsessed with Pokemon and Michael Jackson. None of his boys would ever believe he used to moonwalk around the house in a Pikachu outfit, and used to cry at the drop of a hat. Anthony is a so-called *'badman'* now, and a *'badman'* doesn't cry, even though I know it's all an act for the streets.

When mum and dad first split, he took it quite badly and started staying out a lot, that's how he first started hanging around with the *T-Field Boys.* At first, it was just on the estate for a few hours here and there, but when mum lost her job for drinking and negligence, because she had forgotten to file some paperwork that resulted in the company losing millions, it was a downhill slope for him. It was a downhill slope for us all really.

Mum was blackballed in her industry and refused to take a lesser pay. She would say, '*I'd rather claim back my taxes from the government in benefits and let your dad do his bit than cheapen myself to a pay cut.*'

I guess she didn't know that the benefits wouldn't pay for a mortgage, and contrary to her beliefs that the system gives out six-bedroom houses, me, her and Anthony ended up on the fourth floor in a two-bedroom flat. Anthony hated having to share a room with me, so he started staying out more and travelling to the countryside a lot. Then he was in and out of jail, I guess that's one way of having your own bed.

Talking of Anthony, I felt a bit of relief to see him walk in just now, but after hearing what he has been told, I'm now thinking this is a whole dream, and I'm about to wake up anytime soon.

I've been telling people for years that this girl is a stalker, and people are only going to listen now because she has tried to kill me. She needs some serious help. You don't even need to be a medical specialist to see. Her eyes always look as if she's seen a ghost and has a walk like Frankenstein. She does loads of weird things when you actually bother to take her in. That's the only thing I don't get about Chenade, how can she not notice her friend is weird?

People say it's just OCD, but I've always known its more than that. People don't notice the crazy eyes as much as me, because of the way she wears her eyeliner. It's hard to tell what she looks like naturally, but I have known her from primary school, so I know, they are the same crazy eyes she's always had. We were never mates, but she has always been weird to me. She used to sit on the bench during playtime and watch me and my friends. Like, literally just stalking us from the benches. Even weirder, whenever she made friends with people it was like she would try to turn herself into them.

I can't explain it, but I remember when she was friends with Letishna, she used to colour a ready circle above her lip and tell people it was a birthmark because Letishna had a burgundy coloured birthmark above her lip. One year she was hanging around with a girl called Ugonnah and all of a sudden, she had an African accent for a year, but no birthmark. Guess why? Ugonnah spoke with an accent and didn't have a birthmark. Trust me, she was weird then and even more weird now.

She used to freak me and Jodie out in primary school. Jodie had told me bare stories about her following her around and the time she had killed her rabbit. I know it is all true because when I lived in my old house, I used to see her on my road all the time and had even caught her looking up at my bedroom window. Her house was the complete opposite direction, which meant, from the location of the school, she would have walked past her own home to get to mine. The day after I confronted her, my cat never came home, and I know she had something to do with it.

Marley, who my dad named after his idol, was given to me as a parting gift, he said that with Marley around I would always feel his presence because the blue-collar Marley wore actually had the stone from his wedding band on it. The cat was my memory of dad, and shortly after the Cat disappeared, so did the connection with my dad, then my house, then my brother and then my mum. That girl jinxed my life and I hate her for it.

And the thing is, I don't get why she wants to be other people so bad; her life looks great. She's definitely not broke. I think she is Angolan on her mum's side and her Dad is Grenadian, my older cousins went to college with him. Despite her parents being dark-skinned, her skin is like honey-mustard with chocolate sprinkled freckles. Her natural hair is the colour of burnt copper and is really thick and kinky. However, she had it straight this morning, so she was looking completely different to how I have described her, her hair looked much darker. She has a squarish face, her jaw bone is very defined, really fishy eyes and an obvious overbite, so she's not necessarily the best-looking, but she is not the worst. She is an only child, with both parents at home. Her dad is a Journalist, he has access to all the celebrities and concerts. Taylor and Chenade are always posting themselves backstage in the VIP areas, I've never even been to a concert. Her mum owns three bars in Central London and she's had a birthday party in each one. She doesn't need looks anyway, she doesn't even need brains, her future is set. That's probably why she and Chenade have a perfect friendship, they both have it all. Even now, after everything she has done to me, I bet her parents and Chenade will be by her side.

Meanwhile, they are going to send me home from here, and who is going to look after me? Eediat Adrianne? She's not even allowed in. But no one cares what happens to Carly.

 'She's a bitch!'

That's what they all say, so, I guess everyone thinks I deserved this because the *'school bitch'* doesn't have feelings, right?

A part of me wishes I hadn't woken up.

THAMESFIELD ACADEMY
DEUR ENIGE MIDDELE WAT NODIG IS

ABOUT THE AUTHOR

Having already self-published an Amazon Best-Selling Children's Book, *'Dressed in Peace'*, Ny M Jones has now turned her writing focus to Young Adult Fiction. After a recent invite to her secondary school Whatsapp reunion group and a discussion about childhood reading experiences that ensued, Ny was left asking the questions: Why did we not read more in our teens? And Where were all the books with Black British Teen leads?

Recalling only a handful in the discussion, with Yinka Adebayo's *'Drummond Hill Crew'* Series and Malorie Blackman's *'Noughts and crosses'*, poignant features, Ny continued her search in the local library and online. She found that despite a surge in the offering of books in the 'Black YA' category, like in her teen years, there were still only a few that had a Black British character list or theme.

Another tail of the discussion for many of the non-readers in the group was around the size of books. With no desire to read, many explained that they were often overwhelmed with the thickness of a book and it was a huge turn-off in them committing to a read.

Armed with this new insight and recollections of stories from her school peers, Ny began to develop characters that were reminiscent of the teens she grew up with and some of her childhood personality, whilst shedding light on social and personal issues present within this audience today.

www.ingramcontent.com/pod-product-compliance
Lightning Source LLC
Chambersburg PA
CBHW070447170726
48291CB00005B/1633